RED NOSE READERS

This Walker book belongs to:

_____

_____

_____

First published 1986 by Walker Books Ltd
87 Vauxhall Walk, London SE11 5HJ
This edition published 2011

2 4 6 8 10 9 7 5 3 1

This book has been typeset in New Baskerville Educational

Printed in China

British Library Cataloguing in Publication Data:
a catalogue record for this book is available from the British Library

ISBN 978-1-4063-3365-7

www.walker.co.uk

Crash!
Bang! Wallop!

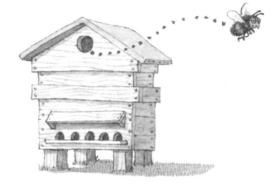

Allan Ahlberg
Colin McNaughton

WALKER BOOKS
AND SUBSIDIARIES
LONDON • BOSTON • SYDNEY • AUCKLAND

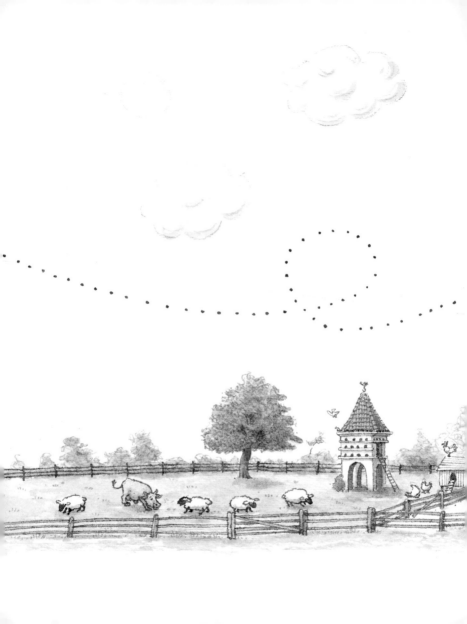

Once upon a time a bee went 'buzz!'

a frog went 'croak!'

a dog went 'woof!'

a sheep went 'baa!'

ten other sheep
went 'baa!' as well,

a farmer went crazy –
and that's not the end of it!

Then his wife
went crazy too,

a cow went 'moo!'

Moo!

a pig went 'grunt'
and 'oink!'

some hens went 'cluck!'

a car went 'beep, beep!'

twenty other cars went
'CRASH!
          BANG!
                    WALLOP!'

and **that's** not the end of it!

Then the farmer went
for the police,

his wife went
to put the kettle on,

Hello! Hello! Hello!

the police said,
'Hello, hello, hello!'
they all drank cups of tea
and that's nearly
the end of it.

Then the sheep came back,

the police went away,

a door went 'slam!'

a baby went 'waaa!'

a cat went 'miaow!'

a bird went
'tweet, tweet!'

and a bee went 'buzz!'
And that **is** the end of it.
Well, almost — except that
once upon a time…

…another bee
went 'buzz!'

Picture
Dictionary

pretty pig

noisy baby

happy dog

sleepy cat

crazy farmer

woolly sheep

busy bee